PRAISE FOR
a current through the flesh

"To call Richard-Yves Sitoski's *A Current Through the Flesh* a tour de force doesn't do the collection justice. Each poem is Yeats' jewel box clicking shut, making intimate everything the reader takes for granted in domestic life: A father's phone call to an estranged son becomes a man shovelling 'water / to fetch a coin at the bottom of a lake', the family dog possesses the ability to 'carry / suffering in its jaws and not puncture it.' Richard-Yves, with measured and effortless concision, reacquaints the reader with the quirks, joys and sorrows that bind family together."
—**ROCCO DE GIACOMO**, author of *Casting Out*

"If *A Current Through the Flesh* doesn't jolt you, you'd better get someone to take your pulse. Richard-Yves Sitoski has written a barn-burner of a family chronicle, full of pataphysical banquets, low-hanging fireworks, and barehanded catches. This book is haunted and just as often hilarious, underscoring the return of what will not leave easily, 'the T. Rex inside the pigeon.' Prepare to be galvanized by this book's wit and grief: this is Sitoski at the height of his powers."
—**TANIS MACDONALD**, author of *Mobile: poems*

"Richard-Yves Sitoski's collection, *A Current Through the Flesh*, is a provocative piece of work, blood spinning around the brain, heart doing acrobatics, soul offering us all sorts of highwire flash. The results are a daring, dynamic vision of domestic dreams gone bad. The red tomato splatter; 'Morning yawns / lips and tongue / stained by pickled beets'; 'I will sink beneath a man / whose hands are shovel blades.' Read *Current* for its mythological fireworks, delicious creepiness and outlandish grasp of imagery standing on its head."
—**BARRY DEMPSTER**, author of *Late Style*

A CURRENT THROUGH THE FLESH

a CURRENT THROUGH THE FLESH

RICHARD-YVES SITOSKI

RONSDALE PRESS

A CURRENT THROUGH THE FLESH
Copyright © 2025 Richard-Yves Sitoski

All rights reserved, including those for text and data mining, A.I. training, and similar technologies. No part of this publication may be reproduced, stored in a retrieval system, or transmitted, in any form or by any means, without prior written permission of the publisher, or, in Canada, in the case of photocopying or other reprographic copying, a licence from Access Copyright (the Canadian Copyright Licensing Agency).

RONSDALE PRESS
125A–1030 Denman Street, Vancouver, BC, Canada, V6G 2M6
www.ronsdalepress.com

Book Design: John van der Woude
Cover Design: Dorian Danielsen
Copy Editor : Kelly Laycock

Ronsdale Press wishes to thank the following for their support of its publishing program: the Canada Council for the Arts, the Government of Canada, the British Columbia Arts Council, and the Province of British Columbia through the British Columbia Book Publishing Tax Credit program.

Library and Archives Canada Cataloguing in Publication

Title: A current through the flesh : poems / Richard-Yves Sitoski.
Names: Sitoski, Richard-Yves, author.
Identifiers: Canadiana (print) 20250211513 | Canadiana (ebook) 20250211521 |
    ISBN 9781553807360 (softcover) | ISBN 9781553807384 (EPUB)
Subjects: LCGFT: Poetry.
Classification: LCC PS8637.I895 C87 2025 | DDC C811/.6–dc23

At Ronsdale Press we are committed to protecting the environment. To this end we are working with Canopy and printers to phase out our use of paper produced from ancient forests. This book is one step towards that goal.

Printed in Canada

For Kim and Sally
in loco parentum

contents

LOW-HANGING FIREWORKS

Low-Hanging Fireworks   3
Things That Don't Show Up in Photos   4
Limitations of Art   5
Yes, Days Are Where You Live   6
Things My Mother Learned Too Late   7
Interlocutor   10
Meteorology   12
Thoughts While Shaving   14
Handyman   15
Courting   16
Baby Boy Sitoski, 3 November 1965   18
Bill and the Rifle   19
Lullaby of the Leaves   20
Anchoress   21
I Asked Him for Water, Lawd, He Gave Me Gasoline   22
A Conversation with the Moon   23

CANADIAN RAISING

Sitowski
Muscle Memory   28
Above All Else   29
Earth Tone   31
Blood Sausage   32
The Denial of Electricity Well into the 1940s
    as a Principle of Domestic Engineering   33

With My Son as Dad Revisits Little Poland, on Hickson
    Avenue Between the CPR and CNR Tracks, Kingston 34
Medicinal 35

Krupa

Universal Character 38
Meanwhile, the Dill Is Bolting 39
A Current Through the Flesh 40
Arrival 42
Short Night's Journey into Day 44
With or Without 46
When a Son Is Born, So Too Is a Father 48
In Lieu of 49

Gratton

Grandpère, dead these fifty years 52
Plank, Nail and Slowness 53
Insignia 55
Mariette, Age Fourteen 56
Stillbirth 57
Photographs of My Mother 60
Astronomy with a Microscope 63
The Seamstress 64
Apron Strings 65

I PLACED A JAR (SLIGHT RETURN) 67

SOMETIMES A MAN

Sometimes a Man   85
Arrival and Departure   86
Ad Astra   88
Lumbering   89
Trestle Bridge Swimming Hole   91
A Guide to Canine Behaviour   92
Snow Angels   93
It's 6:30 a.m. Somewhere in the World   94
Peaches en Regalia   96
Question Mark   98
House Lights   99
Phone Call to My Fifteen-Year-Old Son   101
Another Poem Titled "Ornithology"   102
While My Wife Is in the Hospital Recovering from a Stroke   104
Plonk   105
Envoi   106

Notes and Acknowledgements   109
About the Author   111

LOW-HANGING FIREWORKS

in death my parents
appear the same size

mother is small
and close

father large
but far away

LOW-HANGING FIREWORKS

Mother counted a rosary of comets,
father dropped the Earth
and watched it roll beneath the couch.
Her music was straight as a prairie road,
his was bent like an elbow to the gut.
He preferred the company of dogs,
she of me when I felt like one.
She arrived with ellipses, he with an interrobang.
She baked with chocolate chips
but I always wound up with raisins.
He taught me to fish but each perch I caught swallowed the hook.
Some nights he played heads like percussion instruments.
Some days her migraines were low-hanging fireworks.
In his last hours he was a derelict house,
the handle dissolving when I tried the door.
In hers she was empty as a cathedral
if everything holy within
had risen and flown away.

THINGS THAT DON'T SHOW UP IN PHOTOS

A woman stands at the sink in rubber gloves. The sharp knives
are invisible in soapy water. A husband's snoring breath

has the quality of pistons on a stopping train. A newspaper
lies open like an unfinished argument near a twitching dog who

catches a doe in his sleep. Cigarette ash on the coffee table,
a wooden bowl of walnuts: bison skulls at the foot of a cliff.

Somewhere a migraine leaches unlikely colours
into our spectrum. Sunlight becomes cruel, unusual.

The blood rushing in her head is a flash flood swamping a chapel.
The choir now singing, now screaming.

LIMITATIONS OF ART

I didn't know you at the end. Did you float to Earth
like milkweed floss or hit the ground hard, Hemingway's

last elephant? Was your death a soft rain, the kind
that slowly fills a barrel, or hailstones on the hood of a car?

Were your eyes at the bottom of a lake, looking up
through silt? Would you have seen me, a shimmer

against the sun? Did you swim from your bed and out
a west-facing window, or did you descend, your ankle

snagged in lines that pulled so fast no one saw you sink?

Answer me, for God's sake. Hearts are at stake.
Your legacy. A faulty ticker, a tarnished watch

losing precious seconds by the day. Its endless chain,
its crown you overwound before going.

The organ you bequeathed. Enlarged.
Defective or full of love, I have no way of knowing.

YES, DAYS ARE WHERE YOU LIVE

in your home, your private anywhere.
Your planet in the linty pocket of the Lord.
If I said its walls were papered in recipes
and its roof shingled with ironing boards,
I'd be trite but not wrong.
Let's call it a studio for anandrous songs.
Or maybe a frosted pumpkin
in your life's scooped-out October.
Or a pink deck shoe, canvas-topped and laceless,
one you can kick off without bending over.
Or the space between blanket and Beautyrest on an unrumpled bed,
or the hollow in the pillow for the Fabergé egg
you place for safekeeping
inside your bedroom's bulletproof case.
Maybe a freezer full of soups, cinder blocks of Tupperware.
A sink to drop your cloth into when washing your face.
You get the picture. Comfortable,
safe, mercifully forgettable.
A place where love, thank God, quit gushing
from your pores at the turn of a handle
as in the days you were a sheet, dripping wet,
wrung damp and rolled slowly through a mangle.

THINGS MY MOTHER LEARNED TOO LATE

a honeymoon is a round trip

at first when you make love
you will gasp with the whole of your body
till you feel the air
pushing the backs of your eyes

sometimes he will be the rain you run through
to get from the car to the house
as if running
will keep you dry

drunk he will chuckle
like an engine that won't kick over
sober he will laugh like a child
pretending to be caught on camera

your husband will think
he could spend the day
with his feet in the stirrups
extruding a dumbbell
through his penis
and still meet the boys for a pint

if he draws a finger across your shoulders
his caress
will rub the dust off your wings
this might be intentional

your husband will cook impeccable steaks
but only as good as the ones you select

do not ask what he does in the basement

later when he fucks you
his teeth will be clenched
as if driving in a storm

one day you will decide
that your husband is a beacon
you will be forever charged with lighting

one day your husband will decide
you have all the complexity of a novel
too long to finish

one day he will ask the sphinx
what looks out the window in the morning
shuts the blinds at noon
and sits in the dark at night?

one day your love
will make its last trip to the vet

that night you will drift into slumber
as gradually
as a species going extinct

and you will realize
that your husband was a place of pilgrimage
you crawled on your knees to reach
but could never get to

but when you try to leave
your husband will be everywhere
like the sound of a single cricket

INTERLOCUTOR

Your memory of her is a call on a land line.

You know it's her, as if she had her own ring tone though it's a rotary phone.

Conversation starts *in medias res*. You can't tell when she starts talking. It's like hearing birds before sunrise. How long have they been singing?

She code-switches in each sentence, speaking the language of her childhood and the language of yours.

It's the same stories over and over. Only later do you realize they vary in the telling. An incident here, a detail there. You must accept there's no definitive version.

Because you're not on a mobile, you can't walk around without hanging up. So you squirm in that uncomfortable wingback, the one nobody uses but which has a buttocks groove from when it was her favourite.

You doodle on Post-its. It's when your mind is elsewhere that she drops her conversational bombs.

You can't see her talking with her hands and realize you're missing a good third of the message.

You look around the room, glad she isn't there to notice how slovenly you live.

You look out the window and spot her in the yard. She is about six years old, talking on a tin can and a string. She pantomimes hanging up. A smile idles for a moment on your lips then does a U-turn. It travels at a crawl back into your chest, passed by something different barrelling north.

METEOROLOGY

i.

The house stood below a line of pines.
Columns, reminders
that empires have a shelf life.
In it a man dozed
on a dusty-rose sofa,

Ozymandias half-sculpted
from a ledge of rock
the colour of pink slips,
morning storms,
and a stripper's frosted lips.

Feet Phentex-slippered,
he let the tabloid slide
from his gut to the floor,
snored his way through noonday,
a cloud scudding, bloated and grey.

ii.

The same house quaked
on nights that never rang with sirens.
It was thunder and biblical rain
on the woman who remained
inside for forty days.

The weather channel blared,
teaching her that sky
was nothing to contradict.
She ventured out between the squalls
to hang the laundry—

blush-coloured slipcovers, socks ratty and grey.
Her wet soles on the concrete flags
left lingering prints.
No sun to vanish them,
they led back the way they came.

THOUGHTS WHILE SHAVING

You left your Brylcreemed adolescence on the floor behind you,
followed Buck into the Klondike and locked the door behind you.

It was anarchists on the monkey bars and partisans on the slides,
but a commissar where you left the chores behind you.

Your father grew with every passing year.
He got big as the Cretaceous, 60 foot of dinosaur behind you.

Marriage swelled the population—but only twice,
Darwin giving good advice to leave no more behind you.

You had love enough to sell but flipped the OPEN sign around,
grabbed a rod and reel and shut the store behind you.

No man is an island, but your son's Bikini Atoll.
A treaty's not the same as leaving war behind you.

HANDYMAN

Father was sweaty
like work socks
in a sauna.

His empty hands
always seemed
to hold a hammer.

To fix his wife
he hauled her up a ladder
so she could learn

why flightless birds
should not jump
from ridgepoles.

COURTING

a Thermopylae of lobster shells
buttered bibs like butchers' aprons
picks sticking in lemon wedges like Pantagruel's pitchforks
and then big bands at the Standish Hall
waltz to jitterbug
his feet like electrons
goosebumps
men who dance this well
are hiding things

*

he catches you on the phone with your brother
speaking in French and cackling
he asks you what's so funny
and laughs when you tell him
though the joke makes no sense in English

*

other couples planned vacations
while you planned the garden
rows of beans and short corncobs
beefsteak tomatoes and chives
dill for pickles and garlic for everything

it will face the south side of a bungalow
in a subdivision that never grew
forever incipient
a song that didn't make the charts
from a band you never heard of

BABY BOY SITOSKI, 3 NOVEMBER 1965

Eight months you sailed in mother's placid sea
till a gale swept you away.

Nothing remains but the name she knit,
the one you wore a single day.

It's been my son's for fifteen years
and he was born for it,

so easily it breathes,
so comfortably it fits.

Washed ashore, we'd know he was ours
by its family pattern, its cable and stitch.

BILL AND THE RIFLE

Dad tells the story of Bill and the rifle.
Like all his stories mere anecdote.
Why someone would have
a .30–06 on a fishing trip
is never explained.
They were three days into La Vérendrye,
the trout New Testament dense
and boats as sparse as leaves on a dying birch.

Can you believe it? Bill grabs his gun
and stands on the beach. It's 4 a.m.!
He wants me to laugh before the climax.
He fires two shots in the air
and yells, Everybody off my lake!
Like all his stories it is not funny.

He doesn't say what happened next,
walking the bush,
last night's rye on his breath.

He doesn't mention
woods full of birds not crying out,
pant legs soaked from undergrowth,
the canopy so green it was black,
and the black so inviting

he almost entered
and let the ferns pull him down
like the fists of drowning men.

LULLABY OF THE LEAVES

I'm tone-deaf, mother would brag,
and it was true. She sang lullabies

to calm herself, but her voice
was a field of stubble.

One night after fighting with dad
she sang herself to sleep.

She dreamed she held a burlap sack
and asked of the sun,

What goes in the bag?
The sun answered and she was content,

for his reply was a melody
beautiful as logic, and it told

of a day when photons
could barge into leaves

without seeking permission.

ANCHORESS

Bricked in for thirty years with crosswords and cookbooks,
where does an anchoress go to retire?

Outside, of course. Once the sun has set
and day's unanswered prayers

have drifted off like infant spiders
on their silken threads
to burn a trillion holes in the nighttime sky.

God bless you.

You were always meant to find
the sledge and chisel beneath your bed.

I ASKED HIM FOR WATER, LAWD, HE GAVE ME GASOLINE

Blues in the style of Howlin' Wolf

Father, Grand Guignol actor, your face an Uncanny Valley
likeness of a man's. Roses in the trash from your last apology,

you hang your head so cocked, so on a bias it looks like you are
dangling from a tonsil. The kid in the middle sits outside,

heart made of hummingbirds and head made of televisions.
Some call it love and some declare it *force majeure*.

It once shone like a polyester nightie but now gives blenders
at Christmas. It is a cryptid in the bush and has no property

but the colour of motel soap. It lives in the anecdote
that Lucifer was God's favourite, and only appears

to those who can catch what all of us miss—the taste
of lard over shortening, reflections of the artist

painted in the sitter's eye, how darkness feels its way
down two flights in stockinged feet, avoiding the creaky steps.

A CONVERSATION WITH THE MOON

The Moon rises dripping
from her bath in the sea.
The Moon reassures me: *Some ships keep sailing
even after they've wrecked.*

The Moon admits to being a low-wattage bulb,
a djembe with a torn head, a 45 rpm spindle adapter.
But she wants me
to be wary of analogies:

Don't liken me to a coin,
she chides. *If a coin, I am the one
in a tankard, press gang
waiting by the door.*

Better yet, she says, *I am your mother's beret on a hook,
and the stars are handprints on the wall
where your father caught himself
each time he stumbled, chasing her.*

Canadian Raising

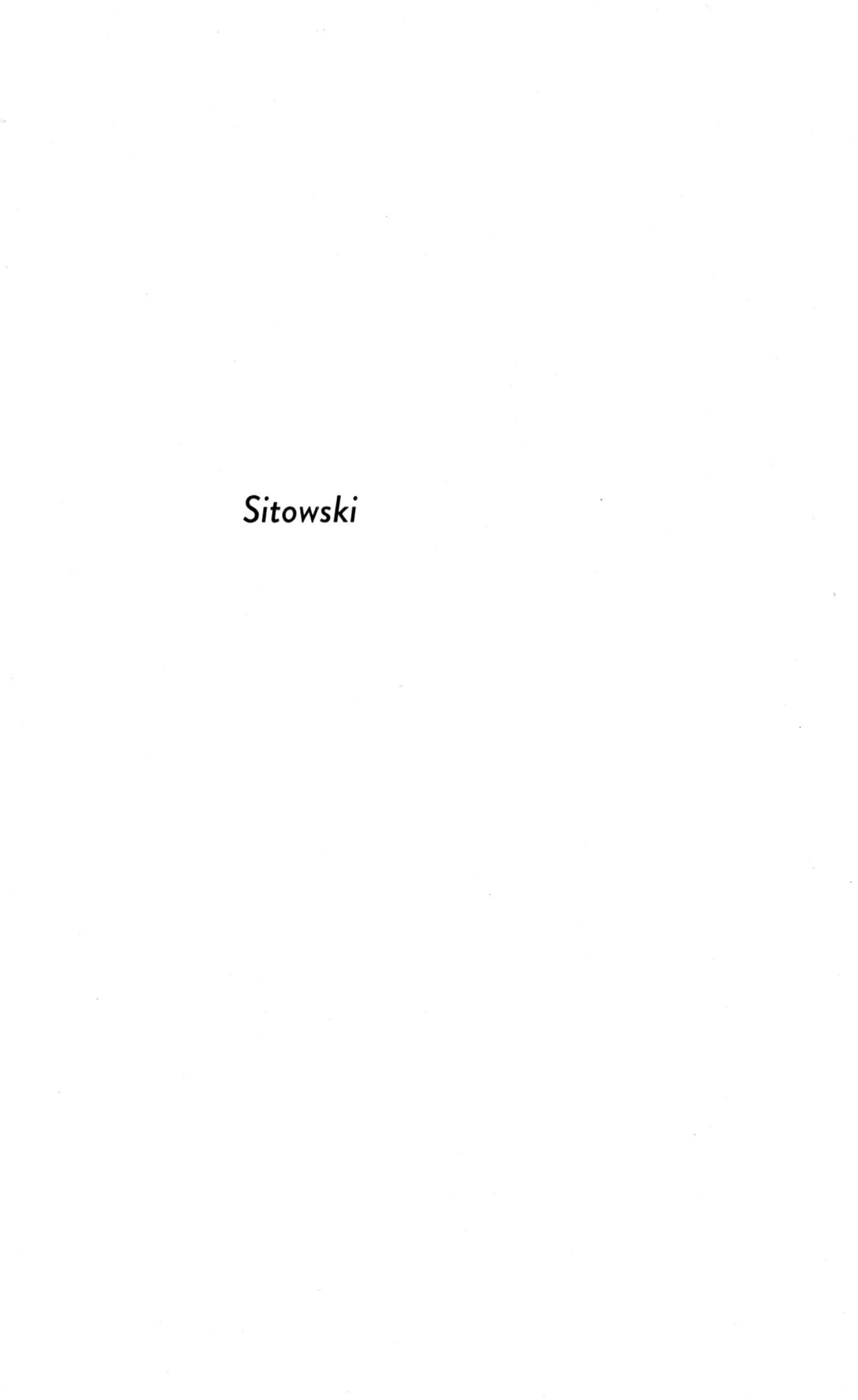

Sitowski

MUSCLE MEMORY

In mem. Józef Sitowski 1884?–1954

Grandfather, the stench of a tannery was your nimbus
as you walked the dirt road home. Till one day you didn't,
your right hand sliced, edgewise, by a splitting machine.

They lifted a flap in your abdomen, stitched fast your hand
to keep the blood flowing. Fused to yourself. All motion stopped
by the knitting of cells, incremental. For months you were Thomas

unconvinced by his own resurrection. You'd as soon rip free
your hand to bring a fist down on the table: one daughter with
a parable inside her, one son using switchblades for a living,

yet another under a tree with books. And three more children
mangled by their own machinery. But you—sitting on a porch
recalling how you once knew horses like your wife knew saints.

How you could swing a strop like a feller his axe. Recalling how
the barn loft was a mountaintop and you spoke in stone tablets.

ABOVE ALL ELSE

a family is what happens to an infant, instantly,
no way to prepare, one minute you're where Buddha lived

when he quit fighting, the next it's thistles and wool socks
and asphalt, coal oil and landlords, tractors and pork fat,

it's a herd of siblings bolting from the table, boys
breaking ranks to flee upwind to jail, across borders, to the

melancholy bush behind the tracks, sisters running into
unloved arms, learning that opinions are a luxury, filling

ashtrays and watching daughters grow oblique to the world,
it's garbles of old country words your parents use around bill

collectors, a language living on as names of foods no-one
in the nursing home has heard of, it's looking through a book on

minerals to find a name for that feeling of you and the shotgun
and the sunrise on the pond, it's stories of a land you will never

visit, populated by giants who fought Panzers on horseback,
it's a father emotive as a moai and a mother with a wind-up key

between her shoulders, it's yesterdays that send your childhood
into exile and todays that close the border, it's never admitting

the fear that bucketwheels your stomach as you stuff pink slips
into bottles and cast them to the waves, it's the wife you argue with

like a dog with a groundhog in its jaws, it's your light, benevolent
as the moon's, when you ask your son why he always comes in

second, it's the son whose search for you has him looking
for your street on a 12-inch globe, it's the genes that inhabit you,

the T. Rex inside the pigeon, pure cerebellum, bipedal appetite
throwing its head full of icicle teeth at innocent herbivores,

thing with feathers that never took to the skies

EARTH TONE

Why mud from Foleyet lumber camps and soot from Pennsylvania
mills and dust from Montana trails would combine—brown, black,

and ochre—on grim Kingston limestone is anybody's guess.
But when you took a shit in the cedar privy behind the house

with no running water, it was on land only lowland crofters
considered blessed. Catholic with a work ethic

in a town where soil was Protestant, you out-Scotted the Scots.
It was a vertical world, and you were only otherwise if someone

knocked you down. Even the cows slept at attention. As for motion,
that was never linear—centripetal swipes of a scythe, the scurrying

of offspring, the arc of a cow's hoof as it kicked an ill-tempered
pail. Each thing came round to its origin. You went to bed

for the purpose of waking up. And the house inched on
through the days, adrift, sails luffing, drawn in circles

by the tired current. You only knew that it was moving
from the ripples in the ground of its foundation.

BLOOD SAUSAGE

he fashioned axe handles
out of seven languages

but English he stacked
behind the shed for kindling

he hired a knife to do
a job he could not abide

proving he was human
and Canadians had uses

THE DENIAL OF ELECTRICITY WELL INTO THE 1940S AS A PRINCIPLE OF DOMESTIC ENGINEERING

A farmer can manage a hundred acres without killing his family. You looked for ways to multiply labour, six children taking turns at rolling Sisyphus's stone. I'll call it ergophilia, your love of work bordering on sexual, in a house a Spartan would call spartan: your wife never knew that electric kitchens were perfected in the '20s. But those were for cities, where pencil-necked architects catered to bourgeois sloth. Still, you had it wrong. How much *more* could she have done with vacuums (patent: 1901) freeing time for chores, how ready for the day would the kids have been with portable fans (courtesy of Tesla, 1890) dispelling the swelter of an August night? Maybe one child would still need to hide in a wardrobe with a book, heart in mouth at each creak from your room. Maybe another would still get pregnant far too soon, another wind up a greaser and die from a syringe. But what was the point of bringing the cold weather in? Why should children learn that fatherly wisdom is too dim to light up a home? Why must a house forever depend on a thing that roars, glows red, and is always being stoked?

WITH MY SON AS DAD REVISITS LITTLE POLAND, ON HICKSON AVENUE BETWEEN THE CPR AND CNR TRACKS, KINGSTON

The return trip was quicker, as return trips always are.
With a slap of cold that felt
like turning away from a fire,
Dad's back in the house where his father believed
in the whisper of cash as it crossed the table.

A house where his mother
was four-square as a dresser shimmed with a crucifix.
A house where the sun would catch its breath
on the whitewashed porch
then collapse on a bed
in a room where summer nights were long.

A house where he was asked,
Why did you name your rabbits?
Did you think they'd escape the block?
and his answer was to put on pyjamas,
which made the empty shape of a boy,
then fall desperately asleep respiring the smell
of heartbroken hay that longs for the scythe.

A house in which I'm having an unclothed moment.
One of those when a father worries enough
to squeeze his toddler's hand,
as if the tighter the grip the safer he could keep him.

MEDICINAL

I have a friend who is convinced
that I suffer the same ailments as her.
She diagnoses us based on YouTube videos
pushing nutritional supplements.
But what I have cannot be cured by collagen.
I've got that thing where you grow up
with a father who hates everyone
including the people he loves.
I cannot remember him before this
any more than recall where I got the notion
that a man once put a straw to his nose
and snorted his father's ashes.
I took my own father's ashes to a small lake on crown land
which was the one place he loved
because there the people he detested ceased to be.
While we fished he'd tell me stories of how my grandfather
killed a distempered dog with his bare hands
and could bench-press 700 pounds.
Sometimes he lectured me on how there were two camps:
on one side the coyotes and hawks
and on the other an endless supply of voles.
At school I lost my lunch money just enough
to know where I sat.
And like that I remember.
It's Keith Richards.
He's the one who medicated with bumps of powdered papa.
This was the story in the schoolyard
and like all such stories it must be true
if only in the way that poems are.

I wish I had saved a dime's worth of Dad to prove it.
I suspect I know what kind of trip it would be.
Euphoric like when the sun abandons gentleness
to bake the green shoots of corn on a pavement of hardpan.
A trip in which you find yourself transformed into a calf
being led into a low brick building.
A trip where you are a gopher shot by a ten-year-old boy in overalls
who bursts into tears over what he's done
though a part of him thinks it's kind of funny.

Krupa

UNIVERSAL CHARACTER

at the age of seven
you train for marriage
watching father
trace letters in the mud
with a willow switch

why do letters have names?
aren't they just the sounds they make?

the youth that you will marry
already signs with an X:

a kiss in the billets-doux
a child gives her mother

fish eyes in cartoons

obliteration on documents

what you carve
on a little cross
above the grave of something gentle
that meant the world
to no one else

MEANWHILE, THE DILL IS BOLTING

That girl with hair like river silt,
how much space will she hold
in that jackdaw's head of his
after summers of cornsilk children

and trees lush with accidents—
those limbs for falling from,
that ground which stops descent—
how much space will she hold

as she weathers down like cedar
while he barely grizzles
like a dog's impassive muzzle?
The envy-coloured fields don't know,

nor does that other girl,
the one she's never heard of,
who was given a pomegranate
in the cool by the mouth of a cave.

A CURRENT THROUGH THE FLESH

Sister, I only wish that Mother were here.
Mother who got from Magda some powder from Lyons.
It made her cheeks the colour of linen that had the sun still in it.
Remember? Bending down for a kiss she lost us
in the light of a benevolent season.
(You must forgive me.
I'm bigger on the tangents than the story.)
Intuition, a half-beat late,
drills the solar plexus with the fist that holds the dispatch:
erupting from the pew while Fr. Casimir went on
about the quality of mercy, I tipped a pot of lilies
and hobbled as I ran. I made it home
as the first big drops began to drub.
Weeping, I held her like a *pietà*.
She gripped the pitchfork still
and her shoes were in a puddle.
But it was her face, tattooed from behind
in the ink of her own blood—the vessels' tracery
a shroud of crimson lace,
her brow a signed self-portrait of our Maker.
I question not his movements,
question not what I am not to comprehend.
What I know is that tomorrow I will feed the geese,
the hogs will get their scraps,
and when the day is done, I will lie in bed
and shut my eyes like cellar doors.

I will sink beneath a man
whose hands are shovel blades
knowing I am condemned to survive,
for only the sky in its immensity
can stop a woman's heart from beating.

ARRIVAL

The night before Maryanna leaves Smerdyna
which barely exists
for Danzig
which has a different name
she lights the coal-oil lamp
and asks what flickers
the light or the dark

When she arrives in Kingston weeks later
in a brown felt cloche
and daffodil flapper dress
the answer comes
expected as chips
in the rims of enamel basins

A husband she hasn't seen
in a dozen years
and in that time
sent two letters
and ten dollars
says nothing

and when she gets to the house
where she will raise six children
he rebukes her
for stepping off the train
clutching a bag of bread and kielbasa

his words a brace of shot geese
tossed on the table
to prove to strangers
whose home they were in

SHORT NIGHT'S JOURNEY INTO DAY

morning yawns
lips and tongue
stained by pickled beets

let my children plant
their right feet first
getting out of bed

the proofing loaves
are gravid bellies

a teaspoon of urine
for the flu

grab the shrieking handle
and pump

I was not married
in a month with "r"
in the name

there's an art
to not spilling a drop

> *blessed art thou*
> *among women*

the cows
are waking
from dreams of bigger stalls

WITH OR WITHOUT

the coolness of the bed's empty side
with its sag down to slats
a plateau-topping lake

you swing your feet up and out
and for a moment
over the void

low in your belly and heavy
mattock or broom?
pickling jar or whetstone?

you settled on bull calf
biada bez dzieci i biada z dziećmi
but may he bring the least misery

you joke to your eldest
lying in will be the best rest of the week
she's old enough not to laugh

his name will be Jan
after your first
dead from smallpox at age three

dead in an old country
and cradled in your arms
until this week

when you will let him go
and ten new fingers will squirm
in your palms

wanderers in the valley of your hands
till you close them
and the mountains fall

WHEN A SON IS BORN, SO TOO IS A FATHER

when my father was born he was small
oddly yet purposely shaped

a tool for a trade
not practised in centuries

IN LIEU OF

You'll know a mother's love by the stains
on her apron. So what does it mean that hers

is bleached clean? Maybe just that she can roll
a tabletop of dough or chop an armload of beets

or halt a desperate chicken to feed her kids
with minimal emotion, a talent shared with cats.

She sighs up the stairs from the cellar,
sack of spuds an obvious cross.

And there she is, beating confessions from a rug
on the porch or scrubbing baseboards and floors

till dirt's a half-remembered slight.
And you, staring, always the dreamer, mouth open

like a turkey, she says, a turkey drowning in the rain.
When she's had enough she sends you out

to fish for marlin, to moil for gold, to follow Jim downriver.
There's no evidence she understands or ever will.

But she accepts and that is enough. Sometimes love
is a thing you catch with bare hands, carefully,

so as not to crush it. A thing to raise in a crate
lined with straw. A thing to feed and feed

though it doesn't grow, or do more than hunker
in the furthest corner of its blanket-covered box.

Gratton

How delicate mother is.
A violin crafted in Cremona,

a bouquet of daisies
someone left on a chair.

Something you didn't see
when you sat down.

GRANDPÈRE, DEAD THESE FIFTY YEARS

I barely knew him
but still I clear a spot

and share my modest lunch
of bread and boiled eggs

for I miss him
the way you miss a person's voice

though you can't recall
a single thing they said.

PLANK, NAIL AND SLOWNESS

Mother was from a town called Alfred,
where love sounded like

the creaking boards beneath a rag rug,
the *horror vacui* of fiddles

or Montréal crackling through a Bakelite cathedral.
A place where young women

knew enough to boil Eden's apples
down to sweet-tart jelly

and young men saw the serpent
as a worm on a hook

meant for soft white catfish lips.
A place with a plain church and ornate Jesus,

where faith was smooth
as the polished face of a tombstone.

A place where the first pink of dawn
was raspberry stained from that morning's picking

and the last red of evening was a spark
that lit the soot that clogged the chimney.

A place where you rose from bed
knowing that dreams were for the sleeping,

your not-quite adulthood jabbed awake
by a sun that pecked like a hen

when you hesitated gathering eggs.

INSIGNIA

At the age of seven you fell
on an open oven door.
Hands and forearms out
you braced for impact,
were still a moment,
then screamed
to light up the house.
The sound after that
was like vines ripped off brick.
They sent for a healer,
a hook-nosed geezer,
possibly Algonquin,
who knew frightening things.
His paste of herbs and mud
smelled rank and felt like acid.
It was meant to stay
till it lifted on its own.
No touching,
no peeling back to see.
You held off a week
then started poking.
You tucked a thumbnail
into hardpan crazing
and flicked off a chunk.
The patch without poultice
felt like flayed muscle
and left a rough scar,
a corroded copper button.

In hospital beds
we are no bigger
than we were as children.
Your eyes,
citrine from jaundice,
look at the bent plastic straw
like it's the last tree on Earth.
You dictate your will
in hepatic delirium.
What comes out is gibberish.
And the smell.
Piercing, astringent—
urine maybe, or a cataplasm
to reverse organ failure,
something they'd slather you in
from crown to soles,
working it deep into skin.
This time you'd wait.
This time it would fall
of its own accord,
leaving your body
the colour of infancy.
It would even fix the spot
you picked off your elbow,
wanting to witness magic,
uncovering instead the pip,
the tiny death's head
you wore for sixty years.

MARIETTE, AGE FOURTEEN

Borax, lye,
rags wrung tight
till your aching hands
have the dead white weight
of scalded pigs.

A school by night
is twice as large
without the kids.

The straw brush
a corpse
in the scummy bucket.

Your screaming knees
livid under gingham.

An arc of suds on the linoleum
beside the desk
you will fall asleep at
tomorrow.

STILLBIRTH

i.

after long journeys your house is altered

things you return to not as you remember

bigger

smaller

different colours

and the people strange

their faces changed

how they look at you

and you'll toss on a bed that feels like a floor

waking to talk with your child in the dark

in a tongue gleaned on the road

and learned so well

you have no accent

ii.

the first a stillbirth

the second yanked your uterus

off its moorings

your body went to great lengths

to explain why children

were good in theory

iii.

afternoons with blinds up

the world so sudden

sidewalks of mothers pushing

strollers triumphant with infancy

how lush these women

in their dresses of wildflowers

and you

Victorian portrait holding your breath

arms like December branches

cradling

the sky's donation of snow

PHOTOGRAPHS OF MY MOTHER

1946

Seated on a stump.
A fashionable winter coat.

The snow holds its finger
to sound's parted lips.

This is life before
life in interesting times.

1966

With your husband by the Welland Canal,
watching a freighter.

You hold his hand
like a banned book.

1969

You raise the kid
while he repairs the house—

who will finish first?
(Trick question.)

1990

Seated on a couch in a funeral home.
You mourn while he stares at next week.

He is a man God made on the Moon,
his nostrils plugged with dust.

1991

A chickadee on a finger
weighs less than memory.

There is happiness
in knowing

where air goes
when pushed by a feather.

1998

Picnic by the Rideau River.
You, me, and your neoplasm.

Hydrodictyon is net-like algae with a septic odour.
Others, like *Synedra*, clog pipes.

The current here is too slow,
can't wash your body where it needs to be clean.

ASTRONOMY WITH A MICROSCOPE

You came from the generation
that put the planets within reach,
Mother, so it's natural
that I looked at your finger
when you pointed at the sky.

Like you, Mother,
I've misgendered
my share of constellations.
At least I try

though there's a haze between
my lens and the night,
product of a forest fire
a whole world away.

Sorry, I cannot lie.

It's vitreous floaters
in my own damned eye,
and the flames are at my feet,
where I lit them.

THE SEAMSTRESS

The October dawn tastes of unburnt dew.
In one room of the cabin snores a man

who even sleeping does not shut up.
A woman who makes perfect clothes

strips herself of hers and dons a bathing suit.
She enters the lake slowly, the inverse of birth.

Her kicks are awkward as she moves a body
settled on because the good ones had been taken.

But still she swims.
It is her and the lake until there is neither.

She swims with no destination, only direction,
for anything worth having lives west of the horizon.

Daylight is a rumour behind overcast.
Morning will be cold and wet as apples in a barrel.

She feels the chill and heads to shore,
tracks sand into the cabin.

With the lights off, she changes in a dimness
that is too loose in places, too tight in others.

APRON STRINGS

You ran toward God armed
with a butter knife. I am so cowed
I am stopped by bead curtains.
You proved the battle's still fought
though there's no grainy footage.
I'd make bonelessness a virtue,
but what I share with octopi
are little squirts of ink. I've always thought
the moon to be larger than the sun it eclipses.
When you slept you held the weight
of the Earth on your closed lids.
I'm the second dog purchased
to keep the first one calm,
but I take the lead in chewing the couch.
Before you got ill, we took walks in the woods
where you pulled on limbs so it looked
like you held hands with trees.
I stop what I am doing to wonder
if the forty days of rain felt guilty
for all the bloated bodies. In the last
picture of you, your mouth was open
and heaven knows what you were saying.
Perhaps that incompleteness is our lot
and the best we can hope for
is to glimpse bright feathers
through the branches. Or maybe you
were saying I could be whole after all,

that what I needed to survive was
all around me—the church basement
sandwiches and cold coffee, that smell
of potted white lilies.

I PLACED a JAR (SLIGHT RETURN)

*A father is someone
you're meant to forgive,*

*or he you, who's to say.
But meeting on the stairs*

*you dodge to your left,
he to his right.*

The elements I most fear:
fire and its opposite.
So your urn, as heavy and black
as the untuned piano
in a convent parlour,
went home to water and wind.

Was the path ever so steep?
Did a pack-a-day man portage
the full thousand metres
through granite, fallen cedars, black mud?

Poison ivy grows thick,
hems tight.
Black flies break their holding patterns
to leverage vulnerabilities,
their bites sending
currents through the flesh.

I could no more commit you
whole to earth
than make leaves
out of humus.

A long time before your pink slip, your report card showing straight F's and marital truancy, toothpick-lipped, mother and I hastily dressed and left. And left. And crafted the art of abandonment like it was sleight of hand and we were David Blaines teaching ourselves to palm an elephant, whose circus sorrow we carried on trains and buses with the restroom stench of departure under vomit-yellow lights or sat with on sticky station benches through the mentholated nights. When we left too quick to pack, where we went was always back.

Memory is a canoe.
Aluminum, stable as a raft.

No spilled-gas iridescence,
just a paddle
and the antonym of sound.

The water as calm
as the brow of a craftsman
as he planes a board flush.

Where we went was always back. Leaving was a state of being, but running headlong into lack is a few bucks shy of freeing with a purse that's full of Kleenex. In the oven there's a dried-out casserole, by the door a half-price jug of Javex to be unpacked with gender roles, and meanwhile you're as tight as paint on a wall. Screaming threats as if we're there, storming up and down an empty hall and beating the brow of an empty chair. You stuff your face in the darkened kitchen and close the pantry door by kicking.

It's the time of fungi
and the bustling green
of ramps on the forest floor.

Tomorrow's Tilley hats
will find Buzz Aldrin footprints
and wonder who ignored
such bounty.

But the overcast is my bagman
for a theft in reverse.

With every real door opened with a kick, letting in frigid air on sweltering summer nights, you close two metaphoric and send the future crying home on its Radio Flyer trike. And so, the worst pain. Between a burin through the palm and a hornet sting on an infant's dozing cheek. You stepped into the room with unholy calm as disturbing as a man chuckling in his sleep, while she, on her right side and sword hand pinned, woke to a man with chisels in his eyes and the underslung jaw of something benthic built to swallow prey twice its size. Sometimes having a pulse is sufficient provocation. We never saw it coming. So much for our vacation.

The path ends at a rocky put-in.
Lichen on the big boulder
like a skin condition,

charcoal from fires,
beer bottle caps
like gold nuggets in a stream.

Wind turns the lake
into a pint glass
carried by a palsied hand:

ripple and froth,
the essential tremor
of water.

We should have seen it coming, this lost East Coast vacation. Never go on a salesman's business calls too close to the brine. Don't expect family values in *la patrie* of the Acadians, don't eat the lobster, don't get conned by reversing falls. It won't be a good time. Percé Rock is crumbling just offshore, the winding roads and postcard piers dissolve in diner grease, and my mother is a whore and she turned me flaming queer. One drunk brings lividity through air-quote "accidents" while another spins dark-web accusations; this one makes a wife commune with pavement, while that one brings a charge of fornication with the mother in a practice known to breeders crossing back or glorified by Gainsbourg in that citrusy little track.

I do not trip,
do not fall on slick stones.

I do not ask the crows
for silence.

They're the only friends
you had,
cronies from the days
of mickeys in backpacks.

I have nothing to toast you with
but the moistness of my breath
and the sweat of my pits,

so like yours,
so briny and alive,
warm to the nose.

Serge's *Lemon Incest* was left to dry out on the sill. We grabbed the Colgate and my K-Way, mom's sweater and migraine pills. Took a taxi from the lobby and made our getaway. Landed hard at the station, waited for the Voyageur from Fredericton to Edmundston. *Trois heures sur Autoroute 2* and seven more to Ottawa. Diesel fumes, a mother and son like a vanquished knight and squire with credit cards as armour and grocery bags for pillage. I buried my face in the *National Enquirer* and watched as the villages passed by, silent in the night, their sodium lights feeble as boxers too punch-drunk to fight.

A Douwe Egberts cloud.
Loons like TV couples somehow in love.

Your fingers thick with worm slime
and cake crumbs of black peat.

You'd gut the catch on a flat rock.

Near bloodless.
Always dead before the knife went in.

Feeble as boxers too punch-drunk to fight—and I'll leave it there, with a simile I'll drive into the ground in my artless art of plowing through what I can't go around. I'm getting better, though. Night no longer falls but drops from day's andropausal lexicon, and memories no longer hop an 8-foot chain-link octagon to crescent kick my crystal jaw and harry my speedbag skull like a flurry of angry moths laying a beat-down on a bulb. As it should be. We've all got too much on our minds to spend our lives staring at frescoes in solipsistic shrines.

The bag of ash is the size
of two human hearts.

It tears badly
so that part of you
flies on the wind,
part of you sinks
in the shallows,
part of you covers my hands.

I plunge them
to the wrists.

This is just to say, when one leaves too quick to pack, where one goes is always back. Back to a man stuffing his face in a darkened kitchen and closing all his doors by kicking. Having a pulse was sufficient provocation, though who could see it coming on our lost vacation, the accusations of crossing the bloodline back as per sicko Gainsbourg in his lemony track? So as all too often, under sodium lights we left by night, feeble as boxers too punch-drunk to fight. And I've set it down earnestly in an artless ode to a man's moral truancy, switchblade-nicked, and our consummate skill in giving him the slip.

I do not stand
with wet hands

nor wipe them
on my pants.

I write your name with water
on the boulder

where it will stay till blotted
by what these clouds release—

a thing that's likened
too often to tears,

a thing that will fall to Earth
till every lake rises,

overflows, and floods
each twisting mud-slick path

I ever followed you down,
and out, and away.

SOMETIMES A MAN

SOMETIMES A MAN

is leaf litter scattered
      on a leg-hold trap

is a boy running barefoot
      through the woods

ARRIVAL AND DEPARTURE

i.

You appeared quickly, the way a bowl appears on a lathe from a
    block of wood.
The ward is a hard place for your first minutes. Birth named for a
    tyrant
takes a range of tools as special as those Dad hauled around in a
    hand-built box of pine.
What I could see above the tenting meant movements of the
    doctor's arm
like a hand plane's back-and-forth. I half expected curls of wood
    to fly.

Your first escape was from the car, totalled a week before by some
    damn fool
gunning from a parking lot. He bawled when your mother
staggered out, you within. That instant, no one knew what you'd be.
Either today's finished bowl, solid on the bench and ready to
    hold the world.
Or something soft and bent, spreading limp and wet on a bed of
    cement.

ii.

I disappeared slowly, a sun going down on a freshwater sea. These
    waves have rolled
since last glaciation, the closest thing to permanence you will know.
You didn't see me a town away, painting pictures of the shore
    to keep perspective
in an abstract life. Then autumn hit full force like a family court
    judgment.
Nothing survives those gales, least of all a flophouse tenant drinking
    from a bog-warm tap.

I think of your birthday legs floured in beach sand,
your hands on the kite spool keeping the future from scudding
    into clouds.
I never meant for you to hold so long. I never meant to wade into
    the lake,
for you to see the bright red flash as I dove and was
    extinguished, a cinder hissing
and steaming and finally out. No wonder you hate the water.

AD ASTRA

It's sweltering, an August noon of fishwife squirrels and a weed-whacking buzz that causes houses to cover their ears. The boy ignores me loudly, tongue of concentration vital to the work of orbiter assembly. It's a practice old as travel. Before there were boxes to Sharpie into cockpits, there were steamer-trunk panzers in desert camouflage and linen-chest chariots in the thick of Roman battle. It seems that Rockwell is equipping space shuttles with snow-cone dispensers and thumbs-up posters *Because space can be very stressful!* The marker squeaks. Dials and rheostats appear, ways to monitor some 7 million pounds of thrust. Droplets of saliva sputter as he makes a blast-off noise and rides controlled explosions, arcing east like a breeze-blown stalk of timothy. My coffee cools while I look for him, 200 miles above, a mote among the stars, streaking through the aether at 28,000 klicks. It's ninety minutes from dawn to dawn and he doesn't know that time is slow down here, has all but stopped. He doesn't know each day I spend an hour at the mirror trying on smiles, hoping to pin them to my lips but the pegs and holes do not align. He doesn't know that I must flag a tow to reach the pad. But he's good. He's got this. He can see the whole blue world from where he is, hurtling happily through the black with not a care in his gentle bones whether some day he'll meet me there. And as for landing, he's got runways across the globe while I have a bed to crater like a crashing Sputnik. Look how gracefully he glides to his ground crew and his press corps, as earthbound I await, wondering if I'll see him before Detroit gets serious about its promised flying cars.

LUMBERING

i.

My heart was the first thing
father built me out of wood.
The work of a master,
as if the tree had grown it.
It was shaped like a drawer
he liked to open, proud
of how neatly it would shut.

ii.

Drive a screw with a chisel
he'd say
*and when you need a chisel
you got a screwdriver.*
Just to be safe
I also keep the latter
impossibly sharp.

iii.

So many reasons
why the actual size of love
is different from the nominal.
So many reasons why
a cut into the grain
tends to bind,
why we call it a rip.

TRESTLE BRIDGE SWIMMING HOLE

From this height the river's aglitter
like the teeth in a spray-tanned face
on *Hollywood Squares*.
When you leap, the air can't bar your way
but water is vindictive,
taking rebar to your soles.
There's meaning in the fact
that you jump all day but never dive,
jealous of the boy whose headlong courage
is tucked inside his beauty.
There's meaning in the fact that you leave him,
cigarette-lipped and lethal,
when the sun walks the crossties west.
You follow it home to parents
whose love pins your sleeve like a sleeping cat.
Each morning you cut your arm off to be free,
each afternoon the Band-Aid
lifts to drift off in the murk
between the smashed-glass surface
and the unseen things that scare you shitless
in the black beneath your kicking feet.

A GUIDE TO CANINE BEHAVIOUR

Dad loved our golden retriever because it was perfect, which means it did as he said. Mom loved it because dogs can carry suffering in their jaws and not puncture it. I loved it because it never ratted on me when I showered suspiciously long. Of course, I did as I was told but Dad never noticed, perhaps because I didn't beg for treats. I shared in Mom's suffering, but I spoke like a dog explaining metaphysics, which meant that she only heard me howl. Dad thought the dog was his, but it was bought for me. Which meant it was really Mom's. The dog protected us from imagined enemies, the ones it barked at from the safety of the kitchen, and taught me everything I know of love, which is something dogs do all too well. After all, a dog's love is undiscerning. Butterflies, coffee tables, cracks in the sidewalk. Some say dogs are better than us, possessing our strengths without our flaws. But loving so much and so hard is surely a failing. Dogs uphold a standard no human can attain. They raise our expectations like those trainers with the cheese-grater abs who say we can look like them if we take out a membership. And no, don't call me a cynic. "Cynical" comes from the Greek word for dog, yet never has there been a creature less cynical than a dog. Dogs are earnest. They're straight shooters, and if they have to shoot you, they'll do it in the face—not plug you from behind like a cat. Which is why I'll stick with cats. If a thing I love is going to kill me, I don't want to see it coming.

SNOW ANGELS

Snow on a cold day
is no good for making balls.
My son throws it anyway,

handfuls of powder
dispersing in plumes.
He does this many times,

enjoying himself,
unaware that madness
is repeating things

in the hope of different results.
Like making snow angels,
which I cannot do.

He falls on his back to show me,
cuts a billowy skirt
and Visitation wings with a wave

of happy limbs.
But it never works for me.
Watch as once again I make the print

of a small, splay-legged thing
scrabbling on its shell,
desperate for purchase.

IT'S 6:30 A.M. SOMEWHERE IN THE WORLD

Sun pokes horizon
gingerly, a tongue
probing a sore tooth.
I am in the park, stuffing
April in a shoebox.

It's under cars and benches,
like this one, where last week
my son saw me not fly a kite.
The wind caught hold
of the juddering lozenge
and yanked it from my hands,
sending it spiralling.

What was I thinking? Could
dowels, tape and newsprint
divert this child who speaks of Bitcoin
and fears no birthday clown?

I have much to offer
a soul in its crocus
and daffodil days
but I can't tell you what.

Every minute
the world is made anew
and I contrive
to be somewhat less than lost.

So though I want
to save this morning's light
till November, when nights
outstay their welcome,
perhaps I'll give it to my boy.

To play with now
or keep for later, when as a teen
he'll need reminding
that dawn is for birds
that truly sing, not shout
each other down
in ridiculous arguments.

PEACHES EN REGALIA

We spread out on the rocky beach
a proper bacchanalia—
cucumbers stuffed with pearls, tins of Scott Expedition peaches,

Tupperwares of dodo pâté and communion sourdough
—and we picnicked in full regalia:
Mom in her flapper dress glittered like moonlight on snow,

I slayed in a Kmart tuxedo,
while Dad with spats, brogues and a Patek Philippe
pumped the piston of a Coleman stove.

He dipped his line in the lake
and snagged a Fiji mermaid by the lip.
He tossed it back. He was after rusalkas and this was a fake.

Mom took out her needles and didn't stop
till she made a cable knit
out of clippings she got from a barbershop.

I hummed old Blind Lemon and toyed with Voyager probes
and full-scale battleships,
played Operation and got gore on my clothes.

Those around us could only stare
at our pataphysical banquet and Dad's siren fishing,
my Delta blues and Mom's sweaters of hair.

It wasn't our fault if our neighbours never got in our groove.
It wasn't our problem if we left them wishing
they weren't too polite to ask us to move.

QUESTION MARK

The warmth on my hand is radiation aspiring to be a blessing.
Something, at least, between bliss and *blessé*. The snow hides

the ground's true intentions. Muskrat tracks are purposeful,
a strict hypotenuse between both arms of the inlet. Two feet

of ice black as the cellar the sun escapes before dawn.
My father with his fingers inside a trout, careful as a dentist.

A pot of chili on the Coleman and armies of ghosts with
empty bowls. Somewhere to my left a woodpecker matches

my heartbeat. Should I ask him whether God, like the stars,
despairs of going unseen by day?

HOUSE LIGHTS

An ekphrasis on two works by Giorgio de Chirico

i. Piazza d'Italia, late 1940s

the greens here include chartreuse
which your father insists
is a term for red

the reds here are the red
of tomato splatter
the other hues
are the colour of bruises

there is no sun
but gas flames and Fresnels
blasting downstage

but not in the distance
where your father rides
a little train homeward

trilby on his head
a pointless screaming match
inside his pigskin valise

ii. The Disquieting Muses, 1916

your mother's head
is egg-smooth and faultless

when the museum guards doze
you approach with pastels

you are skilled
and draw the marionette
into full-blooded life

your strokes are organic and irregular
imprecisely precise
like a hand-lettered sign

distinctive
the way Europeans
add ascenders to the numeral 1

loving and beautiful
like the handwriting
of an early generation

the cursive in your birthday cards
where she signed
on your father's behalf

PHONE CALL TO MY FIFTEEN-YEAR-OLD SON

You're reading the *Communist Manifesto*, you say,
so I make a joke:
Spoiler alert—they die at the end.
I like this so much I use it for
On the Origin of Species and the New Testament.
Silence tells me I've gone too far,
not-very-bon mot beat into the ground,
dad humour landing
like a can falling from a bag
onto a loaf of warm bread.
Which is me all over, filling space
while you respond with ellipsis dots.
And anyway, who on earth talks on phones?
Just us, it seems. You and the man
you haven't hugged since you were six,
the man who will shovel water
to fetch a coin at the bottom of a lake.

ANOTHER POEM TITLED "ORNITHOLOGY"

apple blossoms tumble and scatter
like contents of a purse
and the sky rejects you too
cardinal chick below my fence
thrashing and thrashing
to gain a foot of loft

you scrape the tops of celandine
flap to exhaustion and drop
growing lesser every time
as Mother frets in a waiting-room daze
and Father's a border guard
pacing with an empty gun

what word for this compulsion
this compound of grief and guilt
that would save the already dead?

we found a budgie when I was twelve
a stray that *thunked* the car
and caught its twig shin in a wiper
a home invader Mom cooked meals for
till we found it cold
legs like canted question marks

wrapped in plastic bags
and left to Wednesday's trash
no albatross around the neck
we simply ate our Swiss Chalet
in the small suburban dusk
Dad crashed before the tube
Mom sewed to stay awake
the house now quiet
and no one found the place diminished
or lights now dimmer
or missed the evening twitter

just so I leave this family to its fate
I wash for lunch
avoiding this display
leaving it all to nature
she who gives to snatch away
she who lets me hop from perch to perch
and sing at mirrors a scant handful of days
before the TV's shut
the books are shelved
and a thick flannel blanket
blackens the world of my cage

WHILE MY WIFE IS IN THE HOSPITAL RECOVERING FROM A STROKE

In this house I enter sleep like a freezing lake, slowly, so that air
isn't knocked from my aching lungs. Toe, ankle, shin.

Then I wake and smash at ice from below.
Friends are sending baskets of fruit

and I couldn't care less about the fate of the world.
When I read, I'm lost amid sign and referent.

Under snow the car is the fake tier of a wedding cake,
and the few brown leaves attached to branches make the trees

look colder still. I miss those muffled walks we took
in pelting sleet, though the bundling up was better

in the way that leaning in can be better than the kiss.
If I'm right, last night had a different weight from the night before.

But which was lighter I cannot say, any more than which
of two spoiling pears I hold in my untrembling hand.

PLONK

I can't tell good wine from bad, let alone this vintage from that.
I'm in awe of my father-in-law, appraising each sip, swirling

the *sang*, the *sangre*, the *Blut* of the gods with a knowing air.
He can find those whiffs of woodsmoke, hints of tobacco.

I try to learn but my mind's not there. Pinot Noir's bouquet,
the product of esters, terpenes and thiols, should, I'm told,

evoke the scent of roses. But only bees remind me
of those, drowsy bees dozing on red silk petals.

I don't get toffee out of port, but hearing the word I see
my grandmother's purse, which makes me think of vinegar.

I've never chewed a bridle, don't know the taste of leather—
not like shock therapy victims clamping down on rawhide

so as not to bite their tongues off. I give up. I defer. No
undertone of plum, no *soupçon* of cherries. I remain a hick, a boor,

that dodgy bore who leaves this life with a bottle in his pants
(a chocolatey Malbec, a fruity Carménère) to stumble vaguely home

and sleep out the sundial in the open heart of a flower.

ENVOI

Mother, born and buried in the same small town,
thanked me at her funeral but we haven't spoken since.
Her loss served me hospital food in a backless gown
but she doesn't understand, could never take a hint.
She doesn't know how frantically I grope
through junk drawers for all that I can find—
elastics, guitar strings, lengths of rope—
to tie to the last three feet of the Fates' red twine.
Meanwhile, so my shrunken head won't swell
and outgrow its flimsy laurels,
Dad's on my chariot and yells
in my ear, *Remember, Caesar, thou art mortal!*
And so I am, in a life where all the words between us
are as simple and direct as what goes on in *Las Meninas*.

notes and acknowledgements

"A Current Through the Flesh": Lichtenberg figures are crimson lightning burns that resemble river watersheds and are produced when capillaries burst beneath the skin.

"With or Without": *Biada bez dzieci i biada z dziećmi*: Woe with children, woe without children.

* * *

Some of these poems have appeared, in different forms, in the following publications: *Shelter in Place*, edited by John O'Neill; *Queen's Quarterly*; *MAYDAY*; *Across the Universe*, edited by Sheila Tucker; *Pinhole Poetry*; the League of Canadian Poets' *Poetry Pause*; my chapbook *How to Be Human*; *Prairie Fire*; *The Windsor Review*; *Train*; *The Fiddlehead*; *RAVEN*; *Barren Magazine*; *Fictional Café*; *The Maple Tree Literary Supplement*; and *Poetry Present*.

Thanks go out to the following for service above and beyond:

The staff and management of the Owen Sound & North Grey Union Public Library, which acts as the steward of both the Poet Laureate program and Words Aloud. Most of all thanks to Library CEO Tim Nicholls Harrison, the Poet Laureate committee, the private sponsors of the laureateship, and all previous and subsequent laureates. You make Owen Sound a poetry town.

Barry Dempster and the Dempster Fire Writers' Group (John O'Neill, Jacquie Dawe, Mollie Coles Tonn, Jaclyn Guldemond) for not letting me get away with anything, anywhere, at any time, under any circumstances—and for doing so in a way that really gets me jonesing to create.

Penn Kemp for being part John Cage, part bird of paradise.

Maryann Thomas of the Ginger Press, who got the ball rolling in 2014.

Allan Briesmaster for his astute editing on the first stage of this manuscript, and for telling me to send it out into the world.

Wendy Atkinson and the team at Ronsdale Press for donning scrubs and being this book's best possible obstetricians.

Happy Serwatuk for detailed analysis of what it means to be third-generation East Europeans eating ourselves stupid on the four Slavic food groups of garlic, guilt, fat and vodka.

Finally, Mary, my human Jack Bush painting, for the Gordian knot of our quantum entanglement; Daniel, for everything he was, is, and will be; to the whole clan of Littles and Merwins for embracing me in the gentlest of kraken hugs; and to my parents-in-law Kim and Sally Little for showing me states of matter beyond the ones I was born to.

ABOUT THE AUTHOR

Richard-Yves Sitoski is a poet, songwriter and performer. He was the 2019–2023 Poet Laureate of Owen Sound, Ontario, on the lands of the Saugeen Ojibway Nation (treaty territory 45 ½). He is co-editor, with Penn Kemp, of *Poems in Response to Peril: An Anthology in Support of Ukraine*, profits from which went to displaced Ukrainian cultural workers, and is the author of the chapbook *How to Be Human* and the full-length collection *Wait, What?*. His one-person musical theatre piece, *Butterfly Tongue*, has played to sold-out houses. He is the Artistic Director of the Words Aloud Poetry Series and serves as Marketing and Publication Coordinator at Kegedonce Press. He lives in Owen Sound with his wife Mary and a thoroughly impossible cat, and uses guitars to make sounds unheard since the Cretaceous.